Can we go outside to play?

Not Today!

Written and illustrated by Jillian Johnston

With special thanks to Jaci Stroud

For Millie and Ali

Millie looked at her shoes by the door and sighed,

'Mummy, can we go outside to play?'

'Not today,' Mummy replied 'we need to stay inside...'

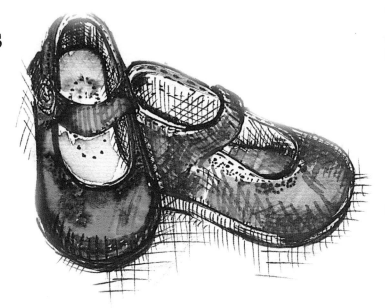

Millie cried, 'But I want to go and play. I want to play in the park!
I want to play on the swings and swing, high in the sky.

I want to go on the slide and I want to go round on the merry-go-round until I'm dizzy and fall down!'

Mummy looked at Millie and smiled. 'You can't go outside today but let's play!

Let's build a park all of our own, let's make it small for Ted!

Let's make a swing with string and put a sun hat on Ted's head!

Let's make a cardboard slide, and a paper plate ride!

We can even paint it too, Ted will have so much fun and your brother, Ali will think it's so cool!

Millie loved her day inside but wondered why?

Why couldn't we go outside she sighed.

So the next day she asked again…

'Daddy can we visit Granny to play?'

'Not today, Millie,' Daddy replied, 'We need to stay inside!'

Then Daddy looked at Millie and smiled.

'You can't go to Granny's today but let's play!

Let's play in our garden here at home!

Let's plant some seeds too.

We can make a fairy garden with a tiny outdoor pool.

Let's decorate stones, add some plants and

make a fairy door!'

Millie claps her hands. Daddy joins and says,

'It's been fun today, playing me and you!

Let's phone up Granny. We can tell her about our garden planted nice and new.

We can talk to her and to Grandad too!'

Millie had a lovely day playing in the sun but why all this stay at home fun?

'It's nursery tomorrow,' she thought. 'Then, I can go out and see my friends to play!'

Tomorrow came. Millie got dressed, had breakfast, put on her socks and shoes.

She waited by the door …

'Mummy, Daddy! ' Millie shouted. 'I really need to go outside today! It's time to play!

I need to go to school!'

'It's the day I go to be with my friends. I learn, paint and sing there too!

I have so much fun, it's the only thing I need to do!

Mummy cuddled Millie, 'Not today, we need to stay inside. There is a bug.'

'A bug? Hmm, I don't like those or slugs.

Don't worry! I'm not scared, I'll pick it up in a cup!

It will go outside... Remember, like the spider we found that time.'

'Not that kind of bug, ' Mummy said sadly. 'This is a virus bug. Do you remember when the doctor said you had a virus?

You were sick with a hurting tummy. This virus can make some people very poorly.'

Daddy added, 'It's a virus bug that you can't see. Lets, keep everyone inside for now in safety!'

'Don't worry….. you'll go out to play soon and see your friends again.'

Daddy and Mummy looked at Millie and smiled.

'You can't go to school today but let's play!

Let's play 'schools' here at home!

Let's ask your brother, Ali to come and join us.

Can Ali be the 'teacher'?

Lets play, what we can learn today?'

Ali raced downstairs, scattering toys and Ted.

'Let's build a fort for the toy soldiers and have an epic battle instead.

Then we can break it, build it again and make the biggest space station to the moon!

I can be the teacher and teach you, Brown Bear and Bonny Dog too!

Let's build our school behind the couch. You get the books, paper and pens and toys and...

Oh... You need to make a spell!

Let's make a potion for the fairies and I need a wand as well!'

I know how to make wands with sticks, ribbons, buttons, glitter, paint and then the fairies will come but don't tell...'

Millie loved her school day with her big brother. What a busy, tiring day!

But.... she really wanted to go outside.

She thought very hard and sighed. Next morning, Millie packed her bag.

She put in her sparkly swim suit, strawberry shampoo and towel.

The swimming pool is not outside, it is inside.

The next day, she asked with a hopeful scowl…

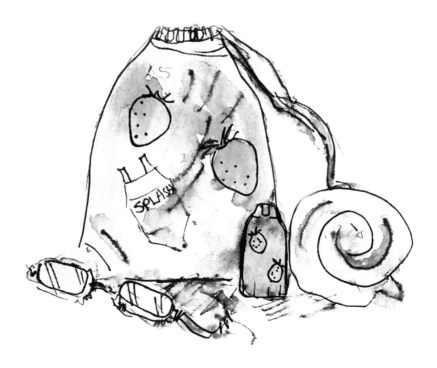

'Mummy! Daddy! Ali! Can we go outside today and play?
We can go swimming. We love to splash and jump and dive!
We can be a starfish or a shark or a seal, lets dance, lets jive!'
Ali shook his head. 'Not today, we need to stay inside…'
Millie exploded in a ball of fire and fury.
'I KNOW THAT! But it IS inside!'

Mummy, Daddy, Ali and Jake, barking loudly, look in surprise.

Ali giggles as Mummy tries to explain. 'Yes, the swimming pool is inside but we have to stay inside our home.

For a while we will stay here together, playing with our paints and games and toys!

It's only for a short time to keep our family and friends safe.

Let's enjoy our special time, just us, as it will be over very soon.'

'Now, let's all think about what we can do.'

Let's get the bubbles, mix them in the bath.

Let's find the goggles, snorkel, floaters, scotty duck and now we're playing at the pool! Splish, splash!

Let's turn the basin into the sea and have sharks and seals, a pirate ship and treasures.

Let's pretend, dress up, write a play which we can perform to Ted and Brown Bear!

The play could be about how we stayed and played inside so everyone stays safe because we all care.

Virus Bug went all around while we look after each other in our homes alone.

Lets all work together to stop it spread.

So yes, sooner than soon and not very long but before your next birthday… you CAN play outside!

You can race in the park and pick apples with Granny, go to school with your friends and play football with Ali.

Let's think of the things we would all like to do when 'inside time' is over and being 'outside' feels like new!

Printed in Poland
by Amazon Fulfillment
Poland Sp. z o.o., Wrocław

57677772R00016